D0359701

Bright and Early Books

Bright and Early Books are an offspring of the world-famous Beginner Books® . . . designed for an even lower age group. Making ingenious use of humor, rhythm, and limited vocabulary, they will encourage even pre-schoolers to discover the delights of reading for themselves.

For other Bright and Early titles, see the back endpapers.

Money, Money, Honey Bunny!

By Marilyn Sadler

Illustrated by Roger Bollen

A Bright and Early Book

From BEGINNER BOOKS®

A Division of Random House, Inc.

For Owen

Copyright © 2006 by Bollen Sadler, Inc. All rights reserved under International and Pan-American Copyright Conventions. Published in the United States by Random House Children's Books, a division of Random House, Inc., New York, and simultaneously in Canada by Random House of Canada Limited, Toronto.

www.randomhouse.com/kids

Library of Congress Cataloging-in-Publication Data
Sadler, Marilyn.
Money, money, Honey Bunny! / by Marilyn Sadler ; illustrated by Roger Bollen.
p.   cm. — (A bright & early book)
"Beginner books."
SUMMARY: Honey Bunny Funnybunny likes to save her money, but also enjoys spending some on herself and being generous with her friends.
ISBN 0-375-83370-6 (trade) — ISBN 0-375-93370-0 (lib. bdg.)
[1. Money—Fiction. 2. Shopping—Fiction. 3. Generosity—Fiction.
4. Rabbits—Fiction. 5. Stories in rhyme.]
I. Bollen, Roger, ill. II. Title. III. Series.
PZ8.3.S13Mo   2006   [E]—dc22   2004023468

Printed in the United States of America   First Edition   10 9 8 7 6 5 4 3

BRIGHT AND EARLY BOOKS and colophon and RANDOM HOUSE and colophon are registered trademarks of Random House, Inc.

Money, money, Honey Bunny!

Thank you, Father.

Thank you, Mother.

Some is big
and some is small.
Does she need
to save it all?

Off she hops . . .

to the shops!

She buys a ball.
She buys a bat.

She buys herself
a pretty hat.

Honey Bunny also spends
on her many, many friends.

She buys a wig
for the pig.

She buys a coat
for the goat.

She buys a pen
for the hen

and a pear
for the mare.

She buys a chair
for the bear

and a trunk
for the skunk.

And oh, what luck
for the duck!
She spent a buck
and got a truck!

She buys some jam
for the lamb

and a blouse
for the mouse.

For the fly
she buys some pie.

For the fox
she buys some socks.

And for the ones
she loves so much,
all the bunnies
in the hutch . . .

She buys some clay
for brother P.J.

and some honey
for sister Sunny.

She buys some candy
for little Andy.

And for her father
and her mother,
she buys some tops
that match each other.

Honey Bunny
gave and gave,

but still has money
left to save!

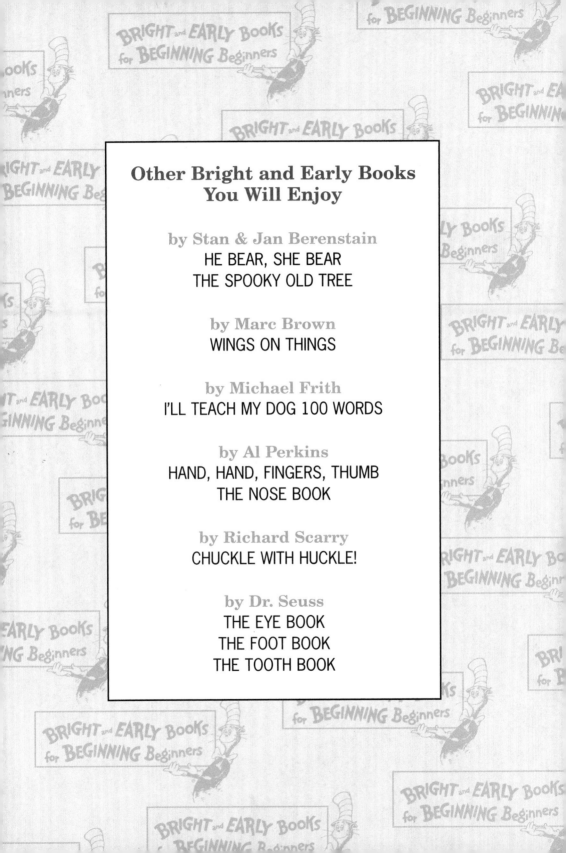

Other Bright and Early Books You Will Enjoy

by Stan & Jan Berenstain
HE BEAR, SHE BEAR
THE SPOOKY OLD TREE

by Marc Brown
WINGS ON THINGS

by Michael Frith
I'LL TEACH MY DOG 100 WORDS

by Al Perkins
HAND, HAND, FINGERS, THUMB
THE NOSE BOOK

by Richard Scarry
CHUCKLE WITH HUCKLE!

by Dr. Seuss
THE EYE BOOK
THE FOOT BOOK
THE TOOTH BOOK